OH BEANS!

St★rring Mean Bean

BY ELLEN WEISS • ILLUSTRATED BY SUSAN T. HALL

Troll Associates

10 9 8 7 6 5 4 3 2

Nobody knew why Mean Bean was mean. Maybe he was just born that way.

His favorite compliment was "Yuck!"

His favorite greeting was "Get lost!"

No one in the world could have been meaner than Mean Bean.

At least, it seemed that way, until one gloomy day in November.

FRIDAY
13

On that day, Mean Bean was waiting at the bus station, pacing back and forth.

He was waiting for his cousin, Extremely Mean Bean, who was coming to visit him.

ARRIVALS TIME
BEAN CITY 3:00
WEST BEAN 3:25
BEANSTOCK 4:12
BEANINGTON 5:15
SAN BEANO 6:33

Finally, Extremely Mean Bean's bus arrived.

"Extremely!" said Mean Bean. "How are you?"

"None of your business," growled Extremely Mean Bean.

"How was your trip?" asked Mean Bean. He was trying hard to be nice.

"What's it to you?" snarled Extremely Mean Bean.

Mean Bean bit his lip. He wanted to scream, but Extremely Mean Bean was his only relative.

BEANT
TX

When they got home, Mean Bean showed his cousin to the guest room.

"It's small and dark," said Mean Bean, getting back to his usual self. "But that's just too bad. It'll have to do."

"FORGET IT!" yelled Extremely Mean Bean. "Move your stuff out of your room. I'm sleeping in there!"

At breakfast the next morning, Mean Bean put a box of Beanios on the table. "There's no milk," he said to Extremely Mean Bean. "So you'll have to eat it dry."

"No way, bub," said Extremely Mean Bean, knocking his bowl to the floor. "Go out and buy me some milk. And some fresh strawberries. NOW!"

"Whew!" thought Mean Bean. "Extremely Mean Bean is even meaner than I am. I'm going to need some help with this."

So he went to see the other beans.

It was hard for Mean Bean to ask for help, but he had no other choice.

He ran into Jelly Bean at the grocery store, and told him about his cousin.

"Meaner than you!" screeched Jelly Bean, tears of laughter rolling down his face. "That's so funny!"

"No, it's serious! You have to help me," cried Mean Bean.

"Okay," said Jelly Bean, giggling. "I think I know just the thing."

SAVE 5¢
SAVE 10¢

That afternoon, while Mean Bean and Extremely Mean Bean were out walking, they ran into Vanilla Bean. Mean Bean introduced them.

"What a stupid hat," said Extremely Mean Bean to Vanilla Bean.

"Why, thank you for your honesty," Vanilla Bean answered. "Perhaps it's time for me to get a new hat, anyway."

Extremely Mean Bean looked shocked.

Next, they bumped into String Bean.

"Nice day, isn't it?" said String Bean.

"What's so nice about it? I think it's disgusting!" yelled Extremely Mean Bean.

"Well, maybe I was wrong. I guess it is a disgusting day," said String Bean.

Then they saw Snap Bean.

"Nice to meet you," he said to Extremely Mean Bean. "We've all been hearing so much about you."

"Lies, all lies," said Extremely.

"Oh, I certainly hope not," said Snap Bean sweetly.

Mean Bean took Snap Bean aside. "Why is everybeany acting so nice to my cousin?" he whispered.

"That's Jelly Bean's plan, you beanbrain," snapped Snap Bean.

"No matter how rotten your cousin is, we're supposed to be nice to him."

In just a few days, Extremely Mean Bean got tired of all the sweetness.

"How can you stand living here?" he shouted at Mean Bean over supper. "Nobody even argues with you! I want to fight with someone!"

The next day, when Mean Bean woke up, Extremely Mean Bean was waiting for him. His suitcase was packed.

"Take me to the bus station," he barked. "I've had enough of your stupid town. Get me out of here! NOW!"

Mean Bean was never so happy to say good-bye to someone in his life. There was only room for one mean bean in Beantown—and that was him.

Later that day, all the beans got together in the Beaneteria for lunch.

"Wow, I'm sure glad Extremely Mean Bean is gone," String Bean said.

"Yes," agreed Vanilla Bean. "I think bean sweet is a lot nicer than bean mean."

"Yuck!" said Mean Bean, completely back to his old self now.

"Oh, well," said Vanilla Bean very sweetly indeed. "Maybe I was wrong. Maybe bean sweet is no good at all."

Jelly Bean winked and agreed, "You're right, bean mean is the way to be."

Mean Bean looked around in shock. Then he realized what was going on.

"You're treating me just as you did my cousin," he said, looking around at everyone. "And if I don't act better, you'll all keep it up, won't you?"

They all nodded.

Mean Bean gulped hard. "I guess," he said, "bean sweet really *is* a lot nicer than bean mean, isn't it?"

Everyone smiled.